THE STREET OF THE FLOWER BOXES

"Who plants flowers on this crumby street?" Carlos protested.
The new family on West 94th Street did and Carlos and his friends
had great fun ripping them up.

When Carlos' grandmother insisted that he apologize to the
Mitchells, he never suspected that they would pay him to be
guardian of the flower boxes. He accepted the job and much more.
Why shouldn't everyone on the block have a flower box for his
window? Carlos took orders from the neighbors and with some
help, made and delivered the flower boxes. The block was in
bloom, but Carlos had not collected enough money to cover his
expenses. How he faces this dilemma provides everyone with a
good time, and the Street of the Flower Boxes makes headlines in
the *Times*.

In his drawings, Peter Burchard captures the shyness and the
energy of the children, their defiance and their fun — just as
Peggy Mann knows them. This lively story about a unique con-
cept of urban renewal could happen in any city — in fact part of
it actually did happen on West 94th Street in New York City.

WEEKLY READER
CHILDREN'S BOOK CLUB

Weekly Reader
Children's Book Club
presents

The
Street of the

Illustrated by Peter Burchard

Flower Boxes

by Peggy Mann

Coward-McCann, Inc.   New York

The Author and the Artist

When Peggy Mann and her husband Bill were married, they wanted to live in a house in New York City. Peggy had grown up in New York and thought that houses were only for "millionaires and movie stars." But Bill had grown up in an English house in the London suburbs. So they began looking.

The result is the charming brownstone where they live today. When they found the house, it was badly run down and located in one of New York's "worst" areas. Long hours were spent working on the house. They got to know the people on the block and to understand the problems in the neighborhood. Much of this involvement in West 94th Street was the inspiration for *The Street of the Flower Boxes*.

Peggy Mann has also written an adult novel and many short stories and articles for national magazines. This is her first book for young readers.

Peter Burchard has illustrated more than fifty books for both adults and children, and is the author of two successful Civil War stories for young people: *Jed, The Story of a Yankee Soldier and a Southern Boy* and *North by Night*.

Mr. Burchard lives and works in New York City.

Library of Congress Catalog Card Number: AC 66-10217

PRINTED IN THE UNITED STATES OF AMERICA

WEEKLY READER BOOK CLUB EDITION

INTERMEDIATE DIVISION

For Mom and Dad

1

"Look!" cried little Luis, pointing.

Carlos looked. Something was happening *again* at the New House. This time a truck had parked in front of it; a truck filled with flowers!

The two brothers ran up the street and stood watching as a fat man in overalls hefted a huge bush down the steps and into the areaway of the New House. Then, returning to the truck, he lifted out a long wooden tray filled with flower pots. He set these out carefully beside the bush, and the brick-paved areaway was transformed into a sudden field of flowers.

"*Caramba!*" little Luis exclaimed with some excitement. "I wonder what's goin' on at this New House *now!*"

7

Actually, the New House was as old as any of the other brownstone buildings on West Ninety-Fourth Street. In fact, for a time it had looked even sadder than the rest of the rundown roominghouses. That was after the fire. All the people had moved out. The broken windows stared like blind eyes. And when the boys on the block climbed inside the building hoping to find a place for a clubhouse, they saw that floorboards had been burned through. Ceiling beams were charred and blackened. And the stinging smell of smoke still hung about the empty rooms.

Then one bright blue morning in April a crew of workmen had arrived at the house: plumbers, plasterers, painters, carpenters. Trucks started pulling up outside to deposit piles of sand, lumber, cement blocks, bricks, bathroom tiles, and all shapes and sizes of wooden boxes and cardboard cartons marked with such words as ELECTRICAL FIXTURE or AUTOMATIC DISHWASHER.

Finally, on the first day of June a gigantic moving van arrived. And the children of the block gathered round to watch men carrying from the van the finest furniture which had ever been seen on West 94th Street.

Then a lady and a man drove up in a taxi and entered the house.

"They sure got a pretty new landlady!" Luis had remarked to his brother.

It was after the lady and man moved in that changes began to occur on the outside of the house. Bright blue shutters edged the windows. Two old-fashioned lanterns framed the front door. And three low brick troughs were built along the side of the areaway. The children made bets as to what these troughs were for.

"To keep goldfishes in," Clarence suggested.

"Some fancy new kinda garbage cans," Carlos had said.

Now, however, the mystery was solved. The man from the flower truck filled the brick troughs with dirt. Then he started planting. Bushes and small trees. Long strands of ivy. And finally an assortment of blossoms which, he told the boys, were called petunias.

"Petooonias?" Carlos said. "What kinda nutty name is that? Petooonias Spitooonias!"

The other children who had come to watch, laughed loudly.

"I think they're pretty!" little Luis said. But he was only five years old and small for his age and no one ever took any notice of his remarks. He was tolerated, in fact, only because he was Carlos' brother.

Carlos was nine. Carlos was tough. Carlos was the leader of the boys still too young to become members of the Big Kings, the official block gang.

9

At times even the Big Kings had been known to follow Carlos' leadership. Especially when he invented games. Walking the Plank, for example. One day he had taken a large beam of wood from the pile of lumber outside the New House. He laid it across the top of two parked cars, and a pirate blindfold was tied over the eyes of each block boy as he teetered his way carefully across the plank. Silly Annello fell off and broke his left arm in three places. But everyone expected something like that from Silly.

Carlos had also invented The Traffic Tieup. Having heard the term on the radio so often, he'd decided to try it out on West 94th Street. He and Clarence collected all

manner of clotheslines and ropes. When night came the
block boys had a fine time tying ropes from the fender of
one car to the door handle of another, parked across the
street. The result was a Traffic Tieup with such splendid
honking and shouting that two squad cars of armed and
helmeted policemen were sent rushing to 94th Street.

Now Carlos invented another game.

When the flower man had driven off in his truck, Carlos
shouted, "Let's play Cat-A-Nine-Tails!"

He promptly pulled out one of the long strands of ivy
and slung it about his head like a lariat, hitting Eddie in
the face with the ivy roots. Some of the dirt went in Eddie's

mouth which was open wide with laughter. Eddie began to cry.

"Whatchu doin'!" Clarence hollered. He was Eddie's older brother. *He* pulled a long strand of ivy from the brick trough, circled it around his head, and banged the roots into little Luis' face.

Then the Battle of the Ivy began. It was followed by the Rain of the Petunia Petals. And when there was nothing left to throw, the boys broke branches from the bushes and tiny trees and chased each other up and down the block screaming with laughter.

The women sitting out on the brownstone stoops, and the men playing dominoes or dice on the sidewalk, watched the boys and laughed along with them. That fine Lady and Gentleman would sure have a fit when they got home and looked into their flower boxes! And it would serve them right. Rich people could do as they wished, of course. But at least they should have sense enough not to show off by moving right in among the poor!

At five-thirty that evening the adults on the block as well as the children were sitting out on the brownstone steps waiting with anticipation until the lady got home. She and the man went off to work every morning. But the lady usually came home first, carrying a bag of groceries.

And sure enough, at five-thirty she arrived. The people of the block kept talking as usual, pretending not to notice her. But all voices fell to a hush as the lady started up the front steps of the New House. Then she glanced into the areaway.

"Goodness!" she said.

She stood for a long moment looking at the pulled-up ivy, the broken branches, the bent flower stalks. the crazy pattern of pink, white, blue and red flower petals crushed against the brick floor of the areaway. Then she glanced at the people sitting on the steps of the neighboring stoop. "Do you know who — did all this?" she asked of no one in particular.

The people stared back at her, impassive.

Finally, Mr. Gonzales said, *"No se, señora."* Mr. Gonzales had been born in Manhattan and knew perfect English. But he answered the lady in Spanish which she obviously did not understand. She smiled a little, or rather she stretched her mouth in a strained, polite kind of way. Then she went on into her house. And shut the door behind her.

Immediately, the street broke into its usual hubbub of sound. The bongo drums began. Mothers leaned out of upstairs windows to call their children. And the general hum of conversation rose like a wall from the people who sat on the stoop steps which, in the spring and summertime, were as crowded as World Series bleachers. On this evening the conversation rose even louder than usual as people reported to each other from stoop to stoop on what the lady had said when she saw her flower boxes.

It was also reported up and down the street that Carlos Gomez and *his* kids had done the damage. No one seemed to blame Carlos; it was simply a part of the News.

The report, however, came to the ears of Carlos' grandmother, who stuck her head out the window to learn what the new commotion was all about. His grandmother was a strict old lady, related in some vague way to a wealthy Puerto Rican landowner. She was proud of her heritage and tried to bring up her two grandsons to be gentlemen. She was reasonably pleased with little Luis. But she cringed inwardly at each report of Carlos' wrongdoings. Outwardly, she reacted by hitting him frequently with a ruler.

The ruler was ready now when Carlos came in for supper. He got a dozen swift strokes on each palm. The strokes were not hard ones, but they were accompanied by a shrilling of Spanish severity from the Grandmother. Then Carlos was told that he must go at once and apologize to the lady for what he had done. Otherwise, he would not get any supper this night, or any other night.

"Listen, Grandmother," Carlos complained. "The flowers were bound to be pulled up by *some*one! That nutty lady should have more sense. Who plants *flowers* on this crummy street?"

His grandmother, who knew little English, did not understand what Carlos had said. Nor did she care. *"Anda!"* she said, pointing at the door. "Go!"

Carlos went.

2

HE WAS NOT exactly afraid as he rang the highly polished brass bell of the New House. But he fervently hoped it would be the lady who answered the door, not the man.

It was the man.

"Hi," Carlos said, looking up. The man seemed much taller than usual.

"Hello," the man said.

"I come to tell," Carlos mumbled, wanting to get it over quickly, "I'm sorry about the flowers."

"Yes," the man said. "So am I. I wonder who did it."

Carlos shrugged one shoulder. Then he shrugged the other shoulder.

"Do you think," the man said, "if we order some more flowers *they* will be ripped up too?"

17

Carlos shrugged both shoulders at once, and flipped out his hands. "People on this crummy block are not used to nice flowers."

"I suppose we could put up a fence," the man said. "To keep the kids out of our areaway."

The lady had come to the door and the man put his arm around her shoulders. "I don't like fences," she said suddenly. "Anyway, it seems to me fences were made to be climbed by children. Right?" Surprisingly, she smiled at Carlos.

He nodded.

"If we get some more flowers," the lady said to Carlos, "would you be their — guardian?"

Carlos frowned, rather suspicious. "What's — guardian?"

"Well," she said, "kind of a mixture of gardener and guard. Part of the job would be to water the boxes three times a week. But the main thing would be protecting the plants. This time we'd get little seedlings. They're not so expensive as the full-grown flowers. You'd have to see that nothing or nobody harmed them so they can grow big. Like the ones we had."

"Your pay," the man added, "would be a quarter a week."

Carlos stared at him.

"Well?" the man said. "How about it?"

Once more Carlos shrugged. "Sure. Why not?"

"What's your name?" the man asked.

"Carlos Gomez."

"We're the Mitchells," the man said. "We'll be seeing you, Carlos."

They shook hands.

Carlos turned, ran down the steps of the brownstone stoop and up the block to his own house. He began to whistle. Not only had he been spared the shame of apologizing, but he had made a deal which would net him a quarter a week. In addition, his grandmother would no doubt be so pleased at the news of his guardian job that she would give him an extra dessert for dinner.

Then, however, another thought hit him. The Big Kings! What would they have to say about it? Especially Angel Andino, their leader. Maybe it would cancel out his future with the Kings, if he took on this crazy job. Protecting *flowers!* He could just hear the Kings laughing over *that!*

3

HE DECIDED NOT to accept the job. After all, his future with the Kings was more important than a lousy quarter a week. (Even though — he reflected quite often — a quarter could buy enough candy to eat yourself sick on. And Carlos was very partial to candy.)

The following Saturday morning, after watching the City Gardener truck arrive and leave, he marched up the steps of the New House determined to tell the Mitchells they had better find someone else to be guardian of their flowers.

The lady opened the door, and gave him that same wide smile.

"Hi!" she said. "Just on time. The plants have arrived.

20

And this too. Your equipment!" She handed him a large aluminum watering can.

Carlos took it.

"If you're free now," the lady said, "let's start in planting the seedlings. Okay?"

Carlos was silent.

"*Are* you free now?" she said. "Otherwise we could do it later in the day."

There was a long pause.

"Is anything — wrong, Carlos?"

He remembered the look on her face when she had first seen her torn-up flower boxes. Somehow he didn't want to ever see her look like that again.

"Sure, lady," he told her. *"Bueno vamos!* That's Spanish," he explained, "for let's get going!"

Some of the kids on the block came around to watch him and the lady do the planting. Certain remarks were made in Spanish. But the lady didn't understand. And Carlos didn't translate.

He did, however, inform the bystanders that he planned to "get" anyone who disturbed the flowers. This remark too was made in Spanish.

"What did you tell them?" the lady said.

"Told them to clear off!" He repeated this sentence in somewhat stronger Spanish words; and with a few further jibes and shoulder shrugs the children moved off. The sidewalk was empty.

The lady had gone inside and Carlos was alone watering down the tiny seedlings and the ivy when Angel Andino appeared. He stood watching for a time in silence. Then he said, "Man, you kill me! Your little silver watering can and all!"

"Listen," Carlos told him, defiant, "if you were given a quarter a week to slop some water on some ol' weeds, would you turn it down?"

"I got a lot better ways to get me a quarter a week," Angel said. Then he walked away.

Carlos watched him sauntering off down the street. There was no way to protect the plants if the Big Kings decided to get them.

Each morning when he woke, Carlos ran to the window. He could see the brick flower boxes from there. And each morning he gave an invisible sigh. The ivy was still in place. No one had disturbed the plants.

It was the same thing at school. Toward the end of the day he got restless, jumpy, wondering whether the Kings had decided to destroy his plants. When the bell rang he would be out of his seat and through the door while the echoes of the schoolbell-clanging were still sounding in the air. And each afternoon he found that his boxes were fine. It seemed like a kind of miracle.

Maybe it was due to the licorice shoelaces.

When Carlos received his first quarter's wages he inquired of Pepe, Angel's little brother, whether Angel liked candy and, if so, what kind.

"Licorice," Pepe said. "Those long twisty kind. Called shoelaces. They really turn him on!"

So Carlos went into Mr. Moriority's candy store on the corner and purchased ten cents' worth of licorice shoelaces which he presented to Pepe.

"For Angel," he said carefully. "With my compliments."

The remaining fifteen cents went for the purchase of assorted sucking and chewing candies which — as a further insurance — he shared with the smaller children on the street.

The system seemed to work, for the flowers remained unmolested.

Furthermore, they grew!

That was the real miracle. In this street littered with the overflow from garbage pails, torn newspapers, and empty cans, these tiny seedlings slowly stretched up green and tall, and sprouted flowers! Just like they were in the fresh-air country someplace. They sprouted and budded like crazy and made fresh new blossoms all through the summer.

What with his high expenses for protection payoffs, Carlos didn't make much profit as gardener. But in fact he didn't mind much. His flowers were doing fine.

Sometimes Clarence and Eddie and others asked if they

could help him tend the brick boxes. But Carlos said firmly, "No!" He felt that he knew each flower and ivy plant personally; each one needed the special care and attention he gave it.

In July his Cousin José-from-the-Bronx came to stay while José's mother was in the hospital having another new baby. Carlos and Luis took him on a tour of the neighborhood showing off the special sights. Saving the best for the

last. They stopped finally by the brick flower boxes at the New House.

"My brother's the gardener at this place!" little Luis announced proudly.

"Yeah?" José said, impressed. He looked at Carlos, who shrugged one shoulder in a modest way.

José-from-the-Bronx stroked one of the pink petunia petals.

"Hey!" Carlos put out a restraining hand. "Stop it, Stupid! Don't you know it'd kill the flowers if everyone started feeling them and pinching them all the time."

"I wish I could be a gardener," José remarked rather wistfully.

"Me too!" said little Luis.

"You can!"

The three boys looked up to see who had spoken.

It was the lady. She was standing by the open window watching them. She smiled. "Come up here, boys. My husband and I would like to discuss something with you."

Carlos went first, marching confidently up the steps of the brownstone stoop. Luis and José followed, holding hands.

It was the first time any of the block children had been inside the New House. At first they just stood still, looking around. There was a piano in the corner. There was a fireplace. A whole wall made of books.

"What's *that* thing?" Carlos said finally, pointing at a bush of glass icicles which hung upside down from the ceiling.

"A chandelier," the lady said. She flicked a wall switch and tiny light bulbs glowed from some of the icicles.

Carlos nodded appprovingly. "Pretty good," he said. "Only it doesn't give much light."

The lady laughed. "Well, that's true. But you can't have everything. Sit down, boys," she said. "I'll get my husband."

They sat, lined up stiffly on the edge of the soft red sofa.

The lady went to the foot of the stairs. "Peter," she called. "We have some visitors."

When the man came down he settled back in the armchair and lit his pipe. "Well," he said, "here's our proposition. It seems that some of the flowers and ivy in the areaway boxes will have to be transplanted into window boxes."

The three boys nodded, though none was quite certain what *transplant* meant.

"As it happens," the man said, "Julie — my wife — and I had already ordered more flowers and ivy for our own window boxes before we thought of this transplanting idea. Our order is arriving today. But if you boys think it's a good plan, I could ring up and get a few extra window boxes. You can transplant some of the flowers and ivy from the areaway. Then each of you can be the gardener for your own window box on your own windowsill. How does that strike you?"

"Sounds okay," Carlos said. (Perhaps his grandmother would know the meaning of *transplant*. But he doubted it, since she knew very little English at all.)

"Well, I'll go telephone City Gardener for the extra boxes," the man said. "That way we'll have yours this afternoon when they deliver our order."

When the man had left, Carlos whispered something in

28

Spanish to little Luis. And Luis immediately piped up, "Lady, my brother say to ask you what means transplant."

"I don't say to ask for *me,*" Carlos explained, reddening. "I thought *they* maybe don't know." He indicated the two younger boys. "And you are better to explain, lady, than me."

"First of all," the lady said, smiling, "my name is Mrs. Mitchell. Or Julie. Not lady."

"Sure, lady," Carlos said. "I understand."

"Well," she went on, explaining it only to Luis and José, "this is what *transplant* means. Take our petunia seedlings, for example. They all grew big and strong. None of them died — which might have happened if they hadn't had such expert care from Carlos."

Luis looked at his brother and grinned with pride. Carlos shrugged one shoulder in a modest manner.

"However," the lady continued, "because *all* the flowers grew so well, the box is now too overcrowded. Some of the smaller plants can't get enough sun or enough nourishment. And they may die."

Luis looked at his brother again, and frowned. Had Carlos done something *wrong?*

But the lady went on in a cheerful voice. "So the thing to do is what all the best gardeners do. Dig out some of the petunias very carefully by the roots and replant them in

29

new window boxes of their own where they'll have plenty of space to grow. And where they can get all the special attention they need from *their* gardeners."

"And that's what is called transplant!" Carlos concluded turning to his brother and cousin, as though he had given the entire lecture.

Mr. Mitchell returned to the room. "Okay!" he announced. "It's all set. City Gardener will be along this afternoon. Suppose you boys ring my bell when you see the truck in the street and we'll get to work."

"Sure!" Carlos said as they rose to go. "Then we will make the transplant."

4

It was three o'clock when the truck filled with potted flowers and ivy pulled up outside the New House. At one minute past three Carlos, Luis, and José climbed the stoop steps. They had carefully kept the secret of the transplanting from the other boys on the block. "Otherwise," Carlos explained, "they'll all want window boxes. And there's not enough transplants to go around."

He was also worried about Angel Andino. Maybe the Big Kings had come to like the look of flowers on their street. Maybe if they saw some extra boxes being made, they'd want them.

"Now, what we got to do," Carlos warned, "is get our boxes onto our own windowsills before those punks is any the wiser!"

He put his finger on the polished brass bell of the New House, and rang.

Mr. Mitchell opened the door and let them in. "Look, boys," he said, "my wife had still another idea. The plastic window boxes which come from City Gardener are all the same shade of green. Julie would like ours painted blue to match our window shutters. I've ordered six boxes for this house. Would you fellows care to do the painting?"

The three heads nodded.

"They'll have to be very carefully done," Mr. Mitchell

said. "The pay," he added, "will be twenty-five cents a box. Okay?"

Again, the boys nodded. "The best of anything I love to do," little Luis exclaimed, "is painting! I never done it before," he added.

Meanwhile, the City Gardener man had deposited in the areaway: four large baskets of earth, eighteen pots of red geraniums, six pots of pink geraniums, twenty-four pots of long, dangling English ivy, and nine green plastic window boxes.

The lady gave the boys a pile of old newspapers which

they spread carefully over the remaining floor space of the areaway. Then she supplied them with three brushes, a large half-filled can of blue paint and a bottle of turpentine.

They began busily to paint six of the green boxes blue.

The secret of course could be kept no longer. Almost immediately, it seemed, every small child in the block had gathered by the areaway of the New House. Even Chico and Ramon, two of the Kings, stopped by to make some sneering comments. But they too stayed to watch.

"We're gonna transplant!" little Luis announced proudly and loudly to no one in particular.

"What's transplant?" Eddie inquired.

"What's the matter?" Carlos straightened up. A streak of blue paint ran from his ear down to his chin. He glared at the gathered crowd. "You don't even know what transplant means? And you supposed to know *English?*"

After that most of the block boys wandered away. Including Chico and Ramon. Maybe because even *they* didn't know the meaning of transplant. They rejoined the stickball game the Kings were playing in the street.

When the three painters had finished their job and had wiped their hands and faces reasonably clean with turpentine-soaked rags, they went inside for their pay and — as it turned out — for lemonade and sandwiches.

"You know, I been thinking," Carlos remarked as he

finished off a peanut butter sandwich. "My favorite color is yellow. Maybe I'll use my twenty-five cents pay to buy me some paint so as I can make my green plastic window box yellow."

"That's a wonderful idea!" the lady said.

"Me, I think I'll paint my window box white!" José said. "White is the cleanest-lookin' color there is."

"I'm having pink!" little Luis announced. "To match my pink geraniums."

"*What* pink geraniums?" Carlos asked.

"There's pink ones. Six pink ones!" Luis insisted. "Outside in the areaway. I counted."

"They're for the lady and man!" Carlos said. "The ones we transplant will all be petunias. "Right, lady?"

"Right," she said. "And wrong. We only have petunias in the areaway. You're right there, Carlos. But my husband and I have decided that we would like some petunias in our window boxes. So if it's all right with you, Carlos, we'll trade some of the geraniums and ivy which came today, in return for some of your transplanted petunias."

"Sure," Carlos replied, rather grandly. "That's okay." He turned to his brother. "There," he said. "Now you can have a couple of pink geraniums if you want to!"

When the last sandwich on the plate had been eaten the

35

boys went on their way to the Columbus Avenue hardware store. Each purchased his own small can of paint. And three more plastic window boxes were transformed: yellow, white, pink.

By the following morning the paint had dried and the boys proceeded with the planting.

This time there was no distracting stickball game in the street and half the neighborhood, it seemed, had gathered around the New House to watch the proceedings.

The crowd parted with something like respect to make way for the three boys as they marched up the areaway steps each bearing his own personal window box filled with geranium and petunia plants and trailing green ivy.

Little Luis stumbled. The box was obviously too heavy for him to carry.

"I'll take that thing for you," Angel Andino said, stepping forward.

"No, you won't!" Luis cried, his voice almost a shriek. "It's *mine!*" Then he added, "Listen, you sure don't want *this* box. You see this green ivy stuff? It's *poison* ivy!"

"Yeah?" Angel said. "Is that right? Well, it looks to me just the same as the stuff the lady's got in her boxes. You mean to tell me she's spreadin' poison ivy around our street?" He laughed a little. "You know something," he said to Luis, "for five years old, you think pretty quick."

Luis glanced around to see whether everyone had heard this compliment; the best one he had ever received in his life.

"Take your box, kid," Angel said grandly.

So little Luis, with Eddie's help, carried the flower box up to the room where he and Carlos lived with their grandmother.

Then, however, a problem arose. The room had only two windows. Each sill had room for only one flower box. Where to place the third?

José-from-the-Bronx offered to keep his box in the corner until he went home at the end of July. Then he would take his flower box with him. But Carlos, who was, after all, the experienced gardener, declared that the flowers would die without sunlight. Since he and Luis were longtime residents of the street it was obvious that *their* boxes should have their place in the sun. "So," Carlos settled the matter of his cousin's window box, "why don't you give your box to Eddie here?"

"Why should I?" José said stoutly.

No one could think of any good reason.

"It's *my* box," José said. I paid for the white paint with my own pay. I planted the flowers with my own work."

"So *sell* it to Eddie!" Carlos suggested. "You can make a good profit. He'll buy the box, won't you, Eddie?"

37

"Sure!" Eddie agreed. "Only," he added, "I haven't any money."

Reflecting then on all the quarters he had been spending at Mr. Moriority's, Carlos decided that the paper-and-candy-store-man must have sufficient funds to buy a window box of flowers. "Let's try him, anyway," Carlos suggested. "We can start off at a high price. Two dollars. We can always come down if he hollers at that."

José had never possessed two dollars of his own all at the same time. With *that* much money he could buy a window box for himself when he got home. Or a racing car game. Or a spaceman's helmet. He agreed.

The procession started off to Mr. Moriority's shop. José went first, carefully carrying his white-painted window box. He was followed by Carlos, Luis, Eddie and a number of other boys from various houses along the street.

Mr. Moriority was enthusiastic about the window box. And his enthusiasm mounted when many of the children stayed to spend pennies on an assortment of candies from his grimy glass case.

"Well!" he announced. "Two dollars. Sure an' that's a good bit a money. But it is, after all, a beautiful-lookin' window box."

He rang open his cash register, took out two crumpled dollar bills, handed them to José, and placed the box in his store window.

When they left the shop the boys noticed that the six blue-painted flower boxes had now been set out on the sills of the New House. They, plus Luis' pink-painted box and Carlos' yellow one, brought a sudden magic to their section of the street. Many people stood looking up, admiring.

Suddenly Carlos turned businessman.

"Hey!" he announced loudly. "Hey, everybody!" Several people turned to look at him. "Anyone want a window

box," Carlos shouted, "he can order it from me! It cost two dollars. Including the flowers and the dirt and the paint job. We paint your box any color you like."

Mrs. Gonzales said she'd take one, painted purple. Mrs. O'Rourke wanted a navy blue with white polka dots. Mr. Henry said he'd have one painted an orangy-red.

Carlos instructed everyone that the money must be paid in advance. Then he ran home to get a pencil and paper for writing down orders, plus an empty cereal box in which to bank the money. And he visited everyone on the block who had shown any interest in having a flower box.

At first, as he took the orders, he felt worried. He actually had no idea how much Mr. Mitchell had paid for each green plastic box and for each separate pot of flowers and ivy. Perhaps a fully planted, individually painted window box cost more than two dollars. But he could not resist the pleasure of writing down the names, making change, stuffing coins and dollar bills into the cereal box.

When he got home and spread all the money on the table he counted up the amazing sum of thirty-two dollars. Sixteen separate orders!

Confident that almost anything could be bought for thirty-two dollars he rang the bell of the New House that evening, the cereal box, now tied up securely, held under his arm.

He explained what had happened.

"Well!" Mr. Mitchell said. "That's fine. Come in."

Again Carlos sat on the edge of the long red sofa. Mr. Mitchell leaned back in his armchair puffing on his pipe. They had a man-to-man business discussion.

Two dollars *was*, it seemed, too low a price for an individually painted window box, plus earth, flowers and ivy.

"However," Mr. Mitchell reflected, "if we could get a good many more orders then we could go to a wholesaler — the man who sells *to* retail stores like the City Gardener. If we could order everything at the wholesale price I'm sure we'd be able to swing it. The same principle applies for the

41

paint. The more orders we have, the larger cans of paint we can buy. And the cheaper this comes out in the end."

Carlos, nodded, agreeing; though in truth he understood very little of what the man said.

"So," Mr. Mitchell stood up, "the most businesslike way to proceed, Carlos, is to canvas the entire block, go from house to house, get as many orders for flower boxes as you can. Then we'll put in such a large order at the wholesaler that he'll *have* to give us a good price. Right? Who knows, there may even be a small margin of profit left over for you and your helpers."

This Carlos understood.

5

THE NEXT DAY, Sunday, Carlos appointed Eddie and Clarence as additional helpers. He gave each boy an Order List which looked like this.

NAME	Adres	BOX color	FLoweRS WANTed STile And color

Each boy also received a Choice List. Every window box would contain two long English ivy and three pots of flowers. The customer could select among:

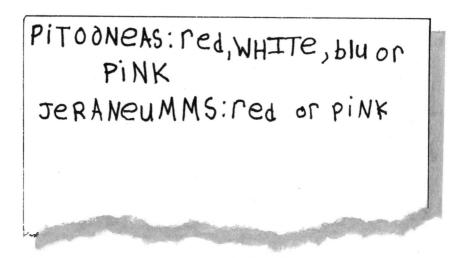

PiTOONeAS: red, WHITe, blu or PiNK

JeRANeuMMS: red or PiNK

Then the boys divided up the houses among them. And each one went from door to door. Some doors were slammed in their faces and some people just weren't interested. One spinster lady kept a yellow-fanged watchdog who sprang out at little Luis growling like a tiger. Luis ran off down the dark stairway screaming and crying.

On the whole, however, most of the people were pleasant enough. Some were even enthusiastic. And by the end of the day the five weary salesmen had collected the stagger-

44

ing sum of two hundred and sixty dollars (including forty-two IOU's dated for the forthcoming payday, or, in some cases, welfare-check day).

Proud and excited Carlos called on his business associate at the New House that evening. He had amassed so much money, so many written orders, that he now carried everything in the battered brown suitcase José had brought with him from the Bronx.

"Well!" Mr. Mitchell exclaimed when Carlos opened the suitcase and sorted out the contents in neat piles on the dining room table. "You've done quite a job!"

When the lady came in and heard what had happened she gave Carlos a hug and a kiss. This embarrassed him a good deal. But, in fact, he didn't mind too much. "You'll change the whole look of our street!" the lady said.

6

THE GREEN PLASTIC WINDOW BOXES were delivered to
the New House on the following Saturday afternoon. One
hundred and thirty of them. Shortly afterwards the West
Side Paint and Supply van drove up and deposited eleven
gallons of paint.

Again, Carlos and his helpers covered the floor of the
brick areaway with a carpeting of old newspapers. The
lady presented them with an assortment of empty coffee
cans in which they could mix the special colors which some
of the customers had specified. She offered to become the
color consultant and during the afternoon as they worked
the boys called in to her through the open window.

"Please, Mrs. Mitchell," Clarence would yell politely.
"How you make orange color?"

"*Missus!*" Luis would holler. "What's to make purple
with?"

But most frequently it was Carlos who called inside: "Hey, lady! We need to consult!"

As the boxes were painted the boys carried them carefully into the cellar of the New House where they were set out on newspapers to dry. Carlos noticed a washer and dryer in the cellar and suggested to the lady that she could earn herself some extra money by opening a neighborhood Laundromat down there. She said that she would consider the matter.

On Saturday afternoon when the painting of the boxes was almost completed the Spinster stopped by the areaway, without her watchdog, and asked timidly whether it was too late for her to order a window box. Carlos informed her that it was. But she looked so crestfallen that he advised her to buy a green plastic window box at the five and ten. "We'll paint it for you," he offered grandly. "And we subtract the cost of the box from your two dollars."

The Spinster said she was most grateful and for her choice of color she selected "a soft baby blue."

She brought the box to Carlos the following day, together with the bill from the five and ten. And for the rest of the week Carlos was deeply worried. The Spinster's green plastic window box had cost $1.39. Of course, he reassured himself, wholesale prices were different from retail. But they would have to be a whole *lot* different in or-

der to be able to sell each box, specially painted, together with five potted plants, for the promised price of $2 apiece!

On the following Saturday afternoon another truck — Maplecrest Nurseries, Growers of Bedding Plants — pulled up in front of the New House. This time adults as well as children crowded about to stare through the slatted back of the old truck.

"Looks like a mountain of flowers in there!" Cincinnati Jones exclaimed.

"*Sí! Muy bonitas!*" Mrs. Gonzales agreed.

Carlos, Luis, José, Clarence, and Eddie helped carry the potted plants into the areaway.

Then Mr. Mitchell came out.

"Have you got the bill?" he said to the Maplecrest Nurseries man.

"Right here, sir."

Carlos watched as Mr. Mitchell took the bill out of its pink envelope, studied it briefly, than stuffed it into his jacket pocket. Carlos followed him inside to the kitchen. "The wholesale price," he inquired, "she okay?"

Mr. Mitchell nodded. "Well, let's get to work!" He took off his jacket, slung it over a kitchen chair. And he and Carlos carried the small kitchen table outside.

The hundreds of color-bright potted plants set out on the floor of the areaway made a sight so splendid that the gathered neighbors stood staring down at the flowers in a kind of awed silence.

Angel Andino and his brother Pepe stopped by to watch.

"Crazy, man!" Angel announced. He was chewing on a licorice shoelace. "They turn me on, those weeds."

"Me too, Angel," Mr. Mitchell said. "They turn me on, too." Then he motioned to Carlos. "We'll set the table here on the sidewalk. This'll be your office, Carlos."

So, exactly as they planned it, Carlos took his seat at the table and Luis and Eddie brought the painted window boxes up from the cellar, two at a time.

"I got a red with yellow dots," Eddie called.

Carlos consulted his order list. "That's Mr. Finney. He gets two ivy. One red, one white, one blue petunia."

Clarence and José filled the boxes with the proper plants, then handed each completed window box up to the team of waiting recruits who were serving as delivery boys.

They worked through the afternoon. The orders were filled quickly, efficiently. Everyone seemed delighted. Except Carlos, who grew more and more troubled about the bill from Maplecrest Nurseries, Growers of Bedding Plants. Finally, he decided to ask Mr. Mitchell straight out whether the money collected did, in fact, cover the costs.

"It's time," Carlos announced loudly, "for a coffee break."

"What's that?" asked Luis.

"Like on that TV commercial, stupid. It means you stop working to have some refreshments."

"Lemonadeansandwiches?" José-from-the-Bronx inquired hopefully. "You suppose she got it ready for us?"

"Listen," Carlos said in a soft voice. "What do you think? She want this whole mess of delivery boys dirtying up her kitchen? You want a coffee break, you go on down to Mr. Moriority's and buy yourself some soda pop!"

The boys promptly departed, all but Clarence who was appointed to keep watch over the areaway, still blooming with an assortment of flowerpots.

Carlos started inside carrying a milk bottle of collected money. "I got to discuss some business things," he informed Clarence.

As he had hoped, it was the lady who answered the downstairs bell. "I come to leave this money with Mr. Mitchell," he announced.

And, as he had hoped, the lady said she would go up and tell Peter that his business partner was waiting downstairs.

Alone in the kitchen, Carlos looked around. Again it happened as he had hoped. There on the sideboard was the pink envelope containing the bill from Maplecrest Nurseries. He glanced around warily like a burglar on TV. Then he took the bill out of the envelope.

It was not as he had hoped at all!

There, in glaring numbers, was the cost of the pots of flowers and ivy, the earth, and the empty boxes. Carlos read it aloud in dismay. TOTAL: $418.43.

He heard Mr. Mitchell's step on the stairs. Quickly

Carlos stuffed the bill back into its envelope and moved.

He was sitting on a stool on the opposite side of the kitchen when Mr. Mitchell came into the kitchen.

"Well!" Mr. Mitchell said. "Julie and I have been watching out the window. It's quite something the way those boxes keep sprouting out on the sills along the street. You've turned our block into a regular garden spot!" The man put a hand on Carlos' shoulder for a brief moment.

Carlos looked up, and, despite himself, he smiled. Then he remembered the bill from Maplecrest Nurseries. Total: $418.43.

Arithmetic was not his best subject at school. He would have to wait for a pencil and paper until he could figure out exactly how much of the bill Mr. Mitchell was getting stuck with. But it was something over the startling sum of one hundred dollars. That much he could figure in his head.

There was something else he could figure in his head.

If he, Carlos, had not been so stupid as to offer the boxes for two dollars apiece; if he, Carlos, had not rushed ahead without so much as consulting his business partner, Mr. Mitchell would *not* have to pay over one hundred dollars to cover Carlos' mistakes!

And what could be done about it? Certainly, the people on the block who had already paid for their boxes could not be asked now for more money. Most of them would, he knew, return their boxes rather than pay more. There would be chaos, commotion, anger on the street, instead of the smiles and good cheer which the flower boxes had suddenly brought to West Ninety Fourth.

"Here," Carlos said abruptly. He handed Mr. Mitchell the milk bottle filled with coins and dollar bills.

"Anything — troubling you, Carlos?"

Carlos shrugged one shoulder. "Troublin'? No? Why?" He stood up. "I better get back to work."

He went outside and took his place at the kitchen-table sidewalk-office. He felt heavy inside as though all the worries of the past week had settled in his stomach like a stone.

53

7

IT WAS WHILE he was concluding the business of the remaining boxes that the idea suddenly hit him.

A number of people had come around during the afternoon to ask whether Carlos had any extra boxes for sale. Obviously, there were still some willing customers. The price could not be increased. But, perhaps, something else could be done.

He called Eddie and Luis to him.

"Listen," he said, "I want you boys to go down the street shouting something. Eddie can shout it in English, and when he's done, Luis'll shout it in Spanish. Okay?"

"Sure," Luis said, proud to have been chosen for this mission. "What we shout?"

"Like this." Carlos suddenly climbed up on top of the kitchen table. "Hey everybody!" he hollered. "One window box will be raffled off for ten cents! One thin dime! Buy your chances here. Ten cents can win you a window box."

Immediately people started coming forward, and Carlos found himself so busy filling out raffle slips that he had to appoint Clarence to take over the regular business of the afternoon.

By six o'clock all the flower boxes had been distributed. And $10.30 had been collected for the raffle.

"Listen," Clarence inquired suddenly. "Both our brothers been hollerin' up and down the street about this here raffle. But we're all out of boxes. Exactly what you planning to raffle off?"

"My own window box," Carlos said, looking up at the ledge where his bright red petunias sat, glowing, it seemed, in the warm summer sunlight. They were certainly pretty all right! His glance traveled then to the other flower boxes set out on the window ledges along the block.

For the first time that afternoon he really *looked* at the street. The Street of the Flower Boxes. It was kind of amazing. Despite the empty beer cans in the gutter, despite the overflowing garbage pails set out on the sidewalk, despite

the litter of crumpled-up newspapers and a soggy, half-burned mattress which had been lying in the street all week, the block really looked like something.

In fact, if you didn't look at the street and gutter and sidewalk, if you raised your eyes to the windows and their brightly painted, flowering boxes, it looked like some beautiful place you might see in the movies or something. You would never recognize it for the crummy old block which had looked like every other slum street in the city.

Carlos climbed up again on the kitchen table, feeling proud.

"Hey, everybody!" he shouted in his loudest voice. "The raffling-off of the window box is about to begin!"

8

L<small>ITTLE-FLEETA</small> M<small>AE</small> T<small>OMPKINS</small> won the raffle.
She'd handed Carlos one of the dimes her mother had given her to buy a loaf of bread. And Fleeta Mae got a sharp slap when she returned home without the bread and only a pencil-scrawled raffle slip to show for her purchases. "When I win the window box," she said looking at her mother, "you'll be sorry for hittin' me."

And, indeed, when Fleeta Mae returned home proudly bearing Carlos' window box Mrs. Tompkins was so pleased that she gave her daughter a sound kiss.

"You were perfectly right, Fleeta Mae!" she announced. "Man cannot live by bread alone!"

"Maybe I should auction off *my* window box!" said little Luis. He was watching wide-eyed while Carlos sat on the bed and counted up the assortment of dimes.

"Yeah," José-from-the-Bronx said dolefully. "What a lamebrain I was! I should of auctioned off *my* box 'stead of selling it to that cluck Moriority for two lousy bucks."

"Listen," said Carlos, "you think I'm keeping this ten dollars and thirty cents for myself? I'm spending it for expenses!"

"Expenses?" José said mystified. "*What* expenses?"

"Punch and cookies. Crepe paper. Things like that."

"Punch? *What* punch?" José exclaimed. "What you talkin', crepe paper?"

"Everyone knows," Carlos said patiently, "you need crepe paper for decorating a street bazaar."

The first items to be festooned with the bright crepe paper streamers were four cardboard inner tubes from toilet paper rolls. These Carlos transformed into megaphones for his Announcement Committee which consisted of Luis, Eddie, Clarence and José-from-the-Bronx.

Every afternoon and evening during the week they paraded up and down the block, as well as through the neighboring sidestreets, shouting into their megaphones: "Come to the 94th Street Bazaar next Saturday afternoon! Celebrate the official opening of the Street of Flower Boxes! Prizes! Refreshments! Games of Chance and Skill!"

But Luis, Eddie, Clarence and José said more than this

59

about the forthcoming bazaar. The remainder of their message was spoken however without the use of decorated megaphones. They told the full story to Mr. Moriority, to Mrs. Gonzales, to Mrs. Tompkins, to Cincinnati Jones, and to others on the block who had seemed particularly interested in the project of the Flower Boxes. Clarence even braved the vicious barking of the yellow-fanged dog when he climbed five flights of sagging stairs to ask the Spinster's cooperation.

"Of course, Carlos got himself into this mess all right," Clarence said as he sat, warily, on the edge of the kitchen chair, his eyes on the chained-up dog. "Still, if he had charged *four* dollars a box at the beginning. probably no one would've bought. Not on *this* block anyway. But now since everybody's all hipped up over their flowers, we figure

why shouldn't they help ol' Carlos to make up the other hundred-and-fifty-eight bucks."

The Spinster agreed that others should, indeed, help. Carlos was at present serving as head of the Refreshment Committee, the Prize Committee, the Games Committee, the Decoration Committee and the Cleanup Committee. This was certainly, she said, too much work for one boy to perform in a week. In a burst of goodwill she volunteered to supply, free of charge, all the pink punch which could be sold during the course of the afternoon.

Then, overwhelmed by her offer, she added hesitantly, "Maybe, I could ask some of my neighbors on this floor to help me. I haven't ever spoken much to any of them. But this would give me a reason."

The following afternoon Mrs. Gonzales knocked on the door of the Gomez room. Grandmother Gomez, after putting on the three chains she always used before opening the door, peered out into the dimlit hallway and frowned in puzzlement.

Mrs. Gonzales was holding an armload of — things. The articles could be described in no other manner.

"For the prizes," Mrs. Gonzales explained swiftly in Spanish. The Grandmother unlocked the three chains, and Mrs. Gonzales entered the room followed by five of her children, each one the bearer of a strange assortment of gifts.

The Grandmother had always held herself rather aloof from the Gonzales. Now, however, her eyes widened, then a smile spread across her face, as Mrs. Gonzales explained that she and her children, upon José's suggestion, had been canvassing the neighborhood all afternoon to collect prizes for Carlos' Street Bazaar.

"He is a good boy, your Carlos," she said in Spanish.

"If he get himself in trouble with the money, it is only right that we help him out."

She directed her children to pile the prizes in the corner. These consisted of a slightly soiled teddy bear, a can opener, a cowboy belt, a World's Fair sweat shirt, a Pan American World Airways calendar, a naked doll three feet tall, a record entitled "Gabriel's Ghost," and various and sundry other items which the citizens of West 94th Street had parted with when they learned from the impassioned Mrs. Gonzales the reason for the forthcoming bazaar.

When Carlos came home that evening and saw the pile of prizes in the corner, he did not smile. He looked, in fact, as though he were going to cry. All he said was, "I didn't even think to ask them to help me. I never ever would've thought they would."

He was not only speaking of the Gonzales. Mr. Moriority had called Carlos into the paper-and-candy shop to say that he would donate paper cups for the punch, plus ten dollars' worth of penny candy to be sold at the bazaar.

Cincinnati Jones had told Carlos he would head the Decoration Committee. "You may not know it, son," Cincinnati said, "but I am quite an excellent painter. House painter," he added after a moment.

Old Mr. Anderson, who had once worked in the City's Sanitation Department, said it was only fitting that he should be head of the Cleanup Committee. "I still got my official uniform," he told Carlos. "I was supposed to turn it in on retirement day, but I got kind of attached to it. So I jus' kept it."

Carlos, long established as an able inventor of games, retained the Chairmanship of the Games Committee. He also went to see the police captain of the precinct to ask whether their block might be shut off as a Play Street on the following Saturday afternoon. It was a strange experience entering the police station of his own free will. It had always been the one building in the neighborhood which he had nervously avoided.

Captain Murphy, however, turned out to be a genial man who listened with great interest when he learned of the crowds of people Carlos was expecting to attend.

"What about the Big Kings?" Captain Murphy asked. "They planning to come?"

"Well," Carlos said, uncertain, "I — dunno."

There was a long pause.

"Tell you what," Captain Murphy said. "Since you're having such a big bazaar, son, I'll do more than close off the street to traffic. I'll assign a couple of mounted policemen to the block. Horses," he added, "always give a little added tone to an affair."

The bazaar was a notable success. Ninety-Fourth Street soon became so clogged with shouting, shoving, screaming children from neighboring blocks that at four o'clock a lieutenant from the mounted police announced that no one else could enter the street, which had been shut off with wooden barriers.

Each separate booth had its own success. There were games of skill: Bop the Cop . . . Push the Pusher . . . Pitching Pennies through the Broken Window. . . . There were games of Chance: . . . Roll the Rocks . . . Spin the Pop Bottle . . . Shoot the Loot.

It was a warm day and the Spinster's punch was consumed so speedily at ten cents a cup that she was kept busy running up and down stairs replenishing the supply while two neighbors worked away in her kitchen squeezing lemons and stirring cans of cranberry juice into the punch, which became more and more watery as the afternoon wore on.

The same excited confusion took place in Mrs. Tompkins' kitchen. She had agreed to supply homemade cookies.

Carlos was kept so busy running around shouting orders,

organizing things, that he had little time to worry about what the Big Kings were up to. Members of the gang were hanging around the different booths, and several times he had noticed them consulting their watches, or asking someone the time.

Carlos expected they were planning a rumble. He was chiefly concerned about making the necessary money before the Kings broke up the bazaar.

At six o'clock it happened, though not in the way he had expected.

A mounted policeman beckoned to him.

Carlos looked up at the cop on the huge brown horse. "Yessir?" he said, both in fear and defiance.

The cop smiled. "Listen son, a couple of people have stopped by the barricades to see whether a riot was going on here. I think it's about time we ended this affair, don't you?"

Carlos stared up in silent surprise. Was the cop asking his opinion, or what?

"Okay with you?" the lieutenant said.

Carlos nodded.

"Good," the lieutenant said. "Captain Murphy spoke to Angel Andino this afternoon to see whether his boys would give us a hand in clearing the street. We're the Bouncer Committee. We've scheduled the Big Bounce for six o'clock.

Right about now." He looked at his watch. Then he gave three shrill blasts on his whistle.

The Big Kings sprang into action. Firmly, quietly, they shoved, pushed, and in some cases pulled, people toward the barricades. Meanwhile, one of the mounted policemen was calling out through a bullhorn, "Please leave the street. The bazaar is over. Thank you for your attendance. Please leave the street now. Please leave the street."

Within fifteen minutes the block was cleared. A brief police-enforced curfew was called while old Mr. Anderson's Cleanup Committee went to work.

During the curfew Carlos sat on the double bed he shared with Luis (and, for the present, with José-from-the-Bronx) and he counted out the money which had been collected. Luis and José stood by watching. The silence stretched with suspense after Carlos reached the hundred-dollar mark.

Carlos kept on counting, quietly. When he had finished he looked up, his face solemn. "We got another problem," he announced. Luis and José stared at him, their eyes wide and solemn. Then Carlos grinned. "We got four dollars and seventy-one cents more than we need! Our problem is what'll we do with it!"

Luis and José let out a shriek. They danced around the room wildly, jumping up and down, hugging each other.

Carlos sat cross-legged on the bed, watching them. And laughing at them. Or at something.

Finally, when the two younger boys had calmed down, they had a business discussion about what to do with the extra money. "I got an idea!" little Luis said. "You could buy yourself a window box!"

"Don't nobody never mention window boxes to me again!" Carlos said. "They made me enough trouble already!"

"Well," little Luis said, "you raffled off your box to make the auction. So I figured —"

"Sure!" José interrupted. "You got a flower box comin' to you. So why not take it?"

Carlos nodded. "Well," he said. "You're right! Why not?"

When the curfew was over he put $158.43 in an envelope and sealed it carefully. Then he went across the street and rang the bell of the New House.

Mr. Mitchell answered.

"Carlos!" he exclaimed. "Come in! That was quite a success, your bazaar! Congratulations!"

"Here," Carlos said. He handed the envelope to Mr. Mitchell. "The deficit money."

"The *what*?"

"*Deficit* money!" Carlos repeated louder, feeling suddenly embarrassed. It was a word he had learned from Mr.

Mitchell during their business discussions. But maybe he had learned the word wrong. "We collected two hundred sixty dollars for the boxes. Right? But the bill came to four hundred eighteen dollars and forty-three cents. I took the bill out of the envelope that afternoon and looked at it. It was wrong to do. Right? But I did it. And I saw there was a deficit. One hundred fifty-eight dollars and forty-three cents. So I figured why should you pay the deficit for my dumb mistake? So we had the bazaar to make up the money. So that's it. In the envelope. One hundred fifty-eight dollars and forty-three cents."

Carlos spoke very quickly and when he had finished, it seemed Mr. Mitchell had not understood one word.

Mr. Mitchell was simply staring at him blankly.

"So," Carlos said, not wanting to go through it all again, "that's it then." He turned to leave.

"Wait!" Mr. Mitchell said.

Carlos waited. He watched as Mr. Mitchell put the envelope into his jacket pocket. "Thank you." Mr. Mitchell said. Then he added, "I have a reporter friend on the *Times*. I told him about our Street of the Flower Boxes. He'd like to come up tomorrow with a photographer. Take some pictures of the street. Interview you and some of your helpers. Would that be okay?"

Carlos shrugged one shoulder. "Sure," he said. "Why not?"

The article was published on the following Tuesday. There was a picture of Carlos and his helpers, and three separate views of the Street of the Flower Boxes. In addition there was two-column story describing how the project had come about and how it had changed not only the look but also the spirit of the block. The story included quotes from the boys as well as Mrs. Gonzales, Cincinnati Jones, Mr. Moriority, Mrs. Tompkins, the Spinster (who, it appeared, was named Miss Lucia Borghese) and old Mr. Anderson (who announced that his Cleanup Committee was continuing on a permanent basis).

A month later a follow-up article was published in the *Times* reporting that a number of people had clipped out the first newspaper story and had stopped by to admire the Street of the Flower Boxes. As a result fourteen more city blocks had now been brightened by window boxes of their own.

Carlos Gomez had supplied the name which headlined the second article. It was called: OPERATION TRANSPLANT.